For Harry and Charlie

ISBN 1 85854 376 2

Published by Brimax Books Ltd,
Newmarket, England CB8 7AU 1996.
Printed in China.

GORF'S POND

by Fiona Hurlock

Illustrated by Eric Kincaid

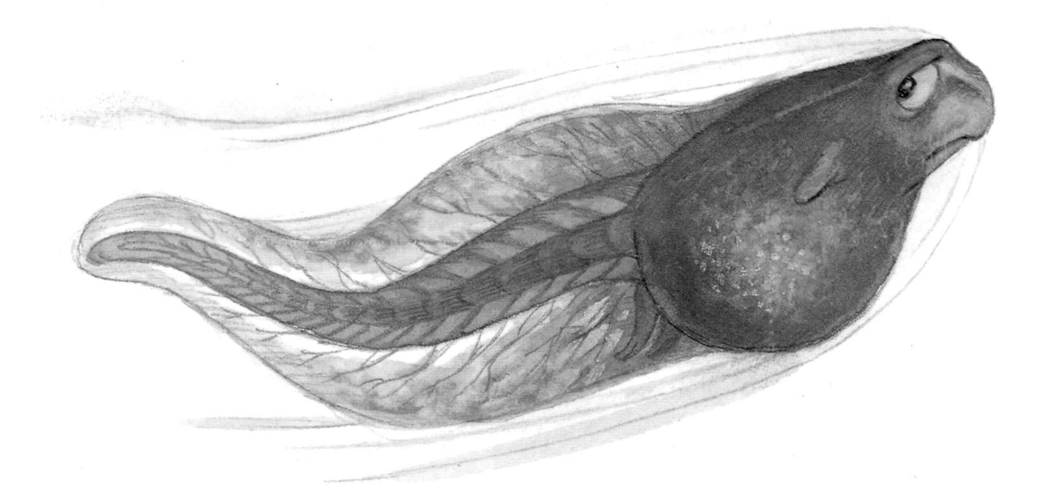

BRIMAX

At the edge of a big field, in a medium sized pond, lived a small fish called Gorf. He lived there all alone with no mother and no father and no friends. Gorf spent all day swimming round and round in the pond looking for something to do or someone to talk to.

One day a bird flew over Gorf's pond and perched on a nearby branch.
"Hello," said Gorf. "Where have you come from?"
"I've flown here from the big pond across the field," said the bird. "That is a very noisy pond with lots of other birds singing. I've come here for some peace and quiet, but your pond is too quiet. I think I'll go back." And off flew the bird.

Poor Gorf. The bird was right. 'This pond is too quiet. If only I could fly to visit the noisy pond,' thought Gorf. But Gorf was a fish and fish can't fly.

The next day a little duck waddled down to the edge of Gorf's pond.

"Hello," said Gorf. "Where have you come from?"

"I've waddled over from the big pond across the field," said the duck. "It's such a busy pond with so many ducks quacking and flapping that I've come for some peace and quiet. But your pond is too peaceful. I think I'll go back." And off the duck waddled.

Poor Gorf. The duck was right. 'This pond is too peaceful. If only I could waddle over to the busy pond,' thought Gorf. But Gorf was a fish and fish can't waddle.

The next morning a bright butterfly fluttered by Gorf's pond.
"Hello," said Gorf. "Where have you come from?"
"I've fluttered over from the big pond across the field," said the butterfly. "It is such a bright pond with so many dancing butterflies that I've come to rest my eyes. But your pond is too dull. I think I'll go back." And off the butterfly fluttered.

Poor Gorf. The butterfly was right. 'This pond is too dull. If only I could flutter over to the bright pond,' thought Gorf. But Gorf was a fish and fish can't flutter.

Gorf spent his lonely days swimming round and round his too quiet, too peaceful, too dull pond, wishing and wishing that he could visit the noisy, busy, bright pond across the field. Gorf spent his lonely nights dreaming that he would grow wings, or legs with big webbed feet, so that he could fly or waddle or flutter across the field to visit the birds and the ducks and the butterflies.

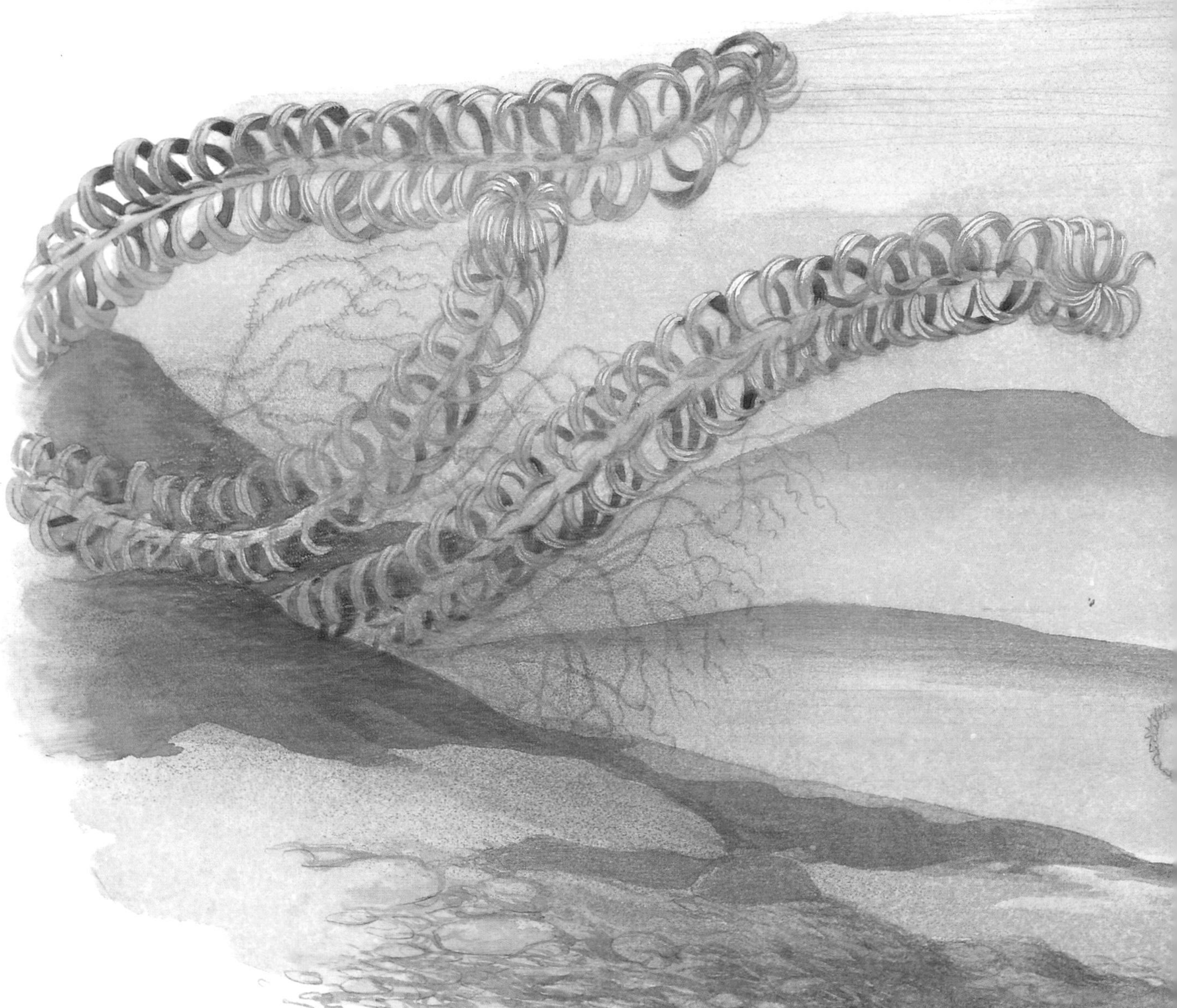

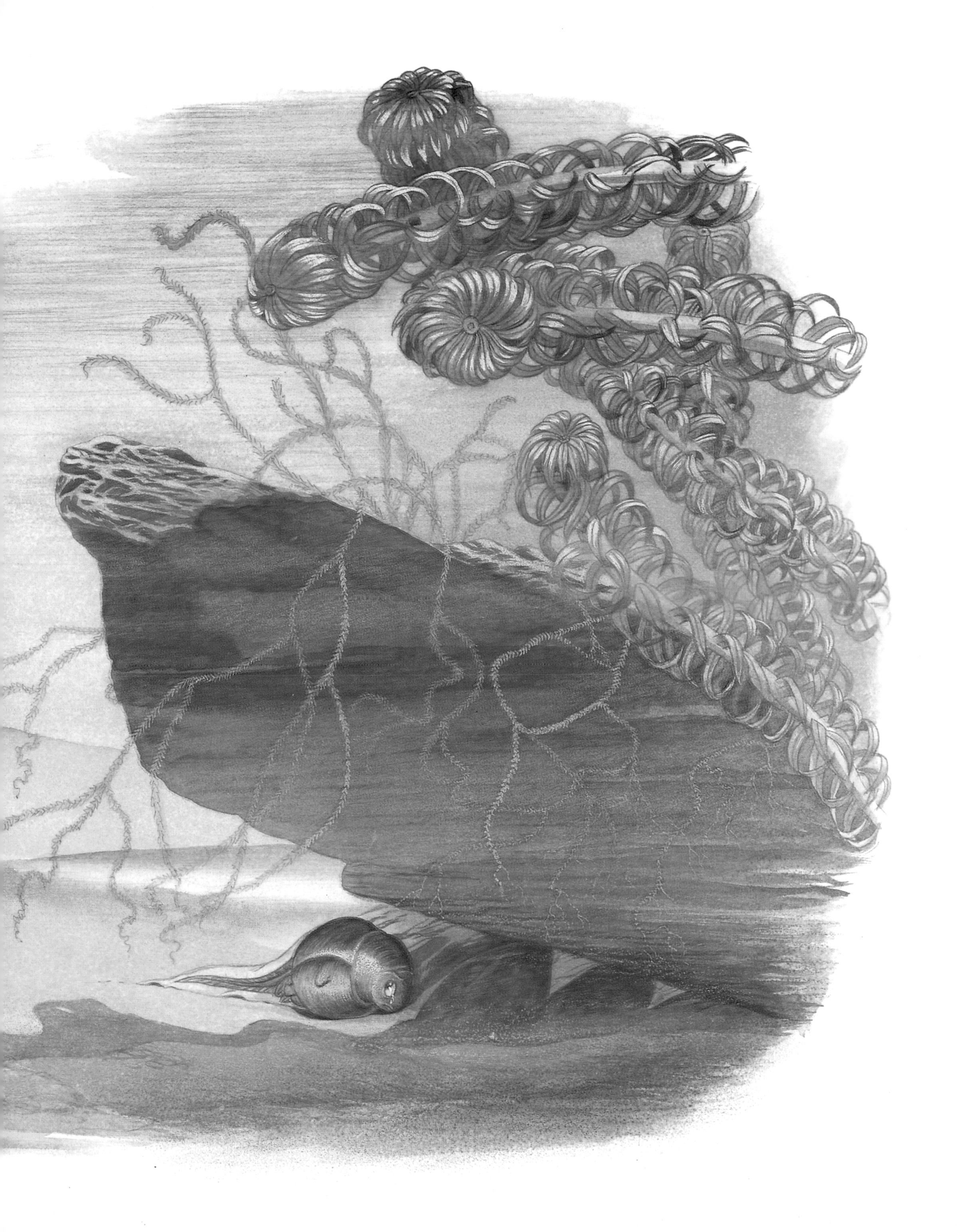

One morning, Gorf woke up with a funny, tickly feeling in his fishy sides. When he looked, he discovered that four little bumps had appeared along his body. Two were below his fishy shoulders and two were above his fishy tail.
Poor Gorf. He didn't know what these strange bumps were and there was no one to ask. 'If only I could go to the noisy, busy, bright pond to visit all my new friends,' thought Gorf. 'They would know what to do.' But Gorf was a fish and he couldn't go anywhere. He could only swim around in his little pond.

Every day the bumps grew bigger and bigger. Then Gorf got a funny, tickly feeling in his fishy tail. 'Oh goodness!' thought Gorf. 'What is happening now?' As Gorf twisted around to see where the funny feeling was coming from, his fishy tail just dropped off!

"HELP! HELP! HELP!" screamed Gorf. "Somebody help me, I'm falling to pieces!" Gorf struggled to the edge of the pond. It was hard to swim without a tail. He shut his eyes tightly. Gorf was scared to look any more. What if something else dropped off? Poor Gorf began to cry. "If only I could go across the field to the big pond," sobbed Gorf out loud. He kept his eyes tightly shut.

"Hello," said a croaky voice. "So you want to go to the big pond, do you? That's where I've come from. There are so many frogs jumping and croaking that it was giving me a headache."
"I need to find someone who can help me," said Gorf. "But I can't go anywhere. I can't fly, I can't waddle and I can't flutter across the field. In fact, I can't even swim as well as I used to because my tail has dropped off!" Gorf began to cry again.
"Why don't you hop across?" asked the voice.
"Because I'm a fish and fish can't hop," wailed Gorf.

The visitor began to laugh, and she laughed and laughed until the tears rolled down her friendly, green face.
"But you're not a fish, Gorf!" she squealed. "Look!"
Gorf lifted his head out of the water. When he at last opened his eyes he saw a strange reflection on the surface of the pond looking back at him. He blinked hard. He looked again and blinked some more.
There, looking back from the pond, Gorf could see a shiny, green frog with big, yellow eyes. The big, yellow eyes were blinking and blinking some more.

“Look Gorf. You’re not a fish. You’re a frog like me!” said Gorf’s new friend.

The bumps on Gorf's sides had grown into two little arms and two big, strong legs. "I'm a frog! YIPPEE! HOORAY! I wasn't falling to pieces after all!" he shouted.
Gorf hopped up and down at the edge of the pond cheering and laughing. "YIPPEE! HOORAY! I'm a FROG!" He was making so much noise that the bird, the duck and the butterfly came to see what all the fuss was about.

"Look at me," shrieked Gorf with excitement. "I'm not a fish. I can hop. Now I can come across the field to visit the noisy, busy, bright pond that you've all told me about."

"Come along then, Gorf," said the bird. "Let's go!"
Gorf was about to hop after the bird when he looked around him. The bright butterfly was fluttering and dancing, the little duck was quacking and flapping with excitement, and the pretty frog was smiling at him and hopping in and out of the water.

"But my pond is no longer too dull, too quiet or too peaceful," he said. "Why don't you all stay here with me instead!" said Gorf. And they did.